THIS BLOOMSBURY BOOK
BELONGS TO

....

With love to Simon,
the Stringston shark

First published in Great Britain in 2002 by Bloomsbury Publishing Plc
38 Soho Square, London, W1D 3HB
This paperback edition first published in 2003

A CIP catalogue record of this book is available from the British Library
ISBN 0 7475 6113 3

Designed by Tracey Cunnell

Printed in Hong Kong by South China Printing Co.

10 9 8 7 6 5 4 3 2 1

Bored Claude

Jill Newton

BLOOMSBURY
CHILDREN'S
BOOKS

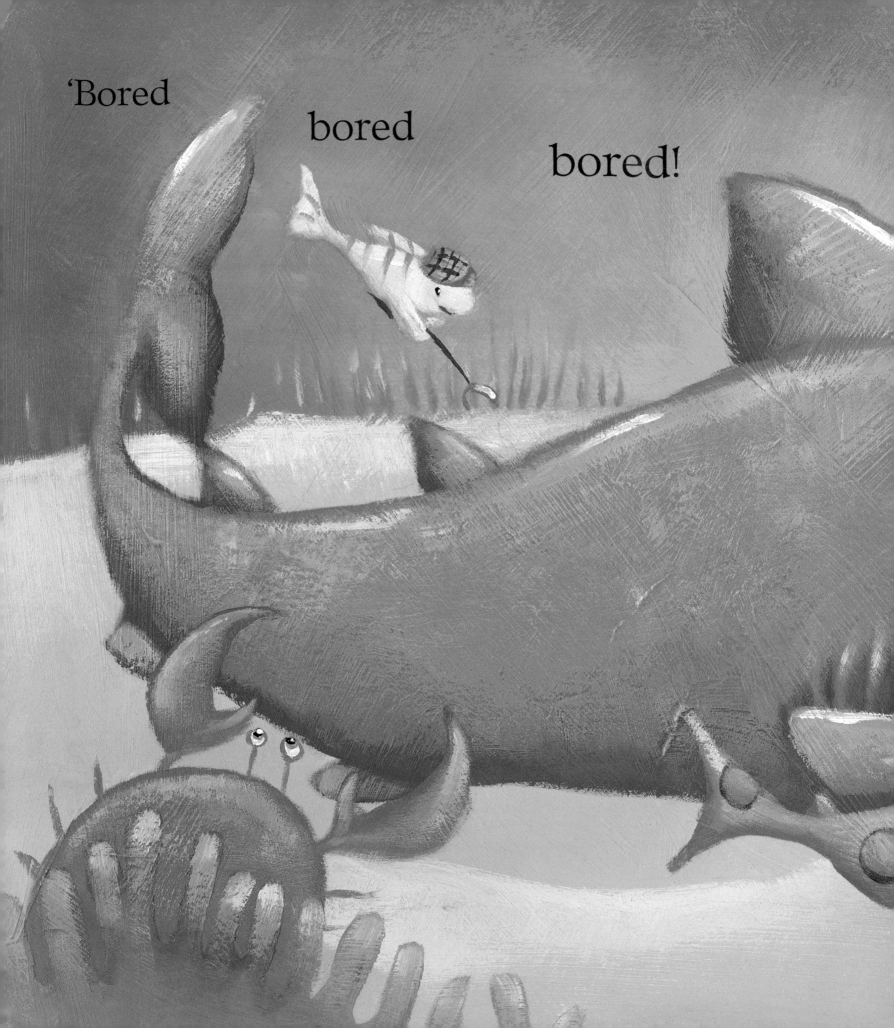

I'm SO bored!'
wailed Claude the shark.

'How can you possibly be bored when there's always so much gardening to be done?' called the fish.
Claude yawned.

'Come and help us hoe!' sang the seahorses.

Claude swam over to hoe,

but soon lost interest.

'Come and help us prune!' clacked the crabs.

Claude swam over to prune,

but didn't really enjoy it.

'Come and help us plant!' waved the octopuses.

Claude swam over to plant,

but planting didn't seem his thing.

'Come and water the flowers!' fluttered the angel fish.

'No!' snapped Claude.
'I'm bored and I'm going home.'

The sea creatures gardened until the sun started to go down, then they swam back to admire the results.

The garden looked stunning!

The next evening the fish held a huge party for all those who had been working so hard to keep the garden beautiful, which was nearly everyone.

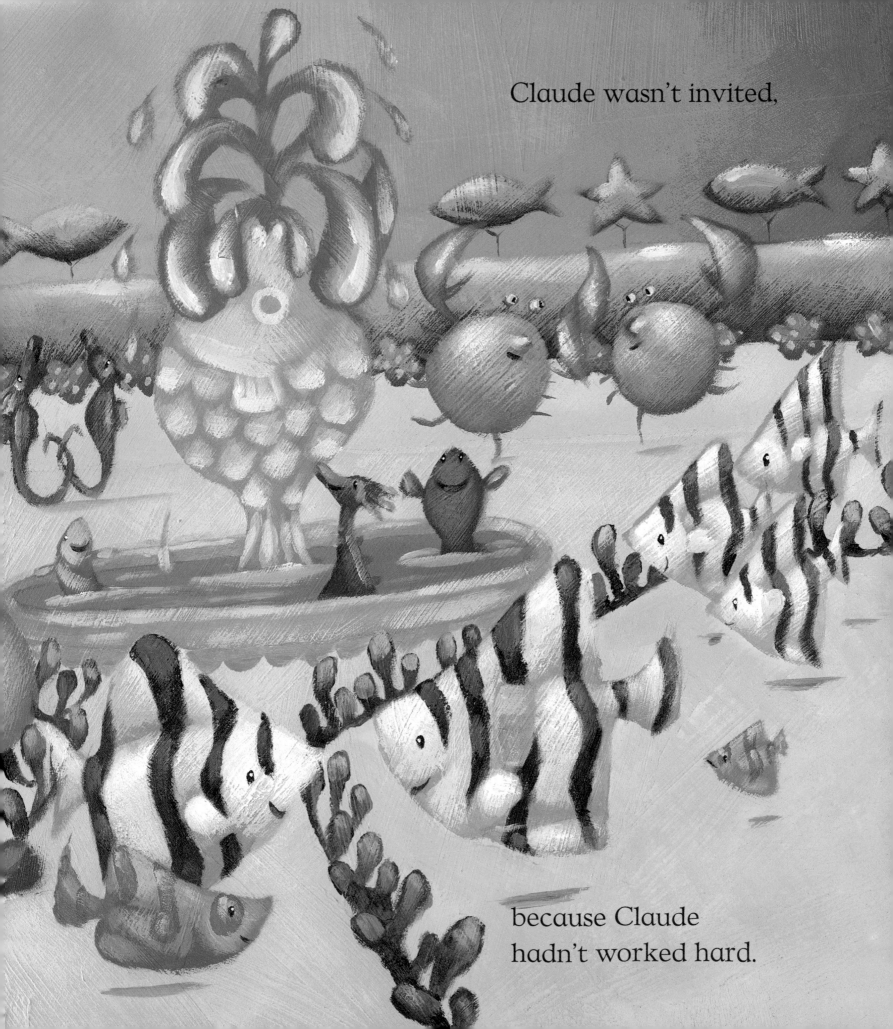

Claude wasn't invited,

because Claude
hadn't worked hard.

Now Claude was

REALLY

bored.

He heard the singing and laughing
and music and felt sad and lonely.

Then he had a great idea!

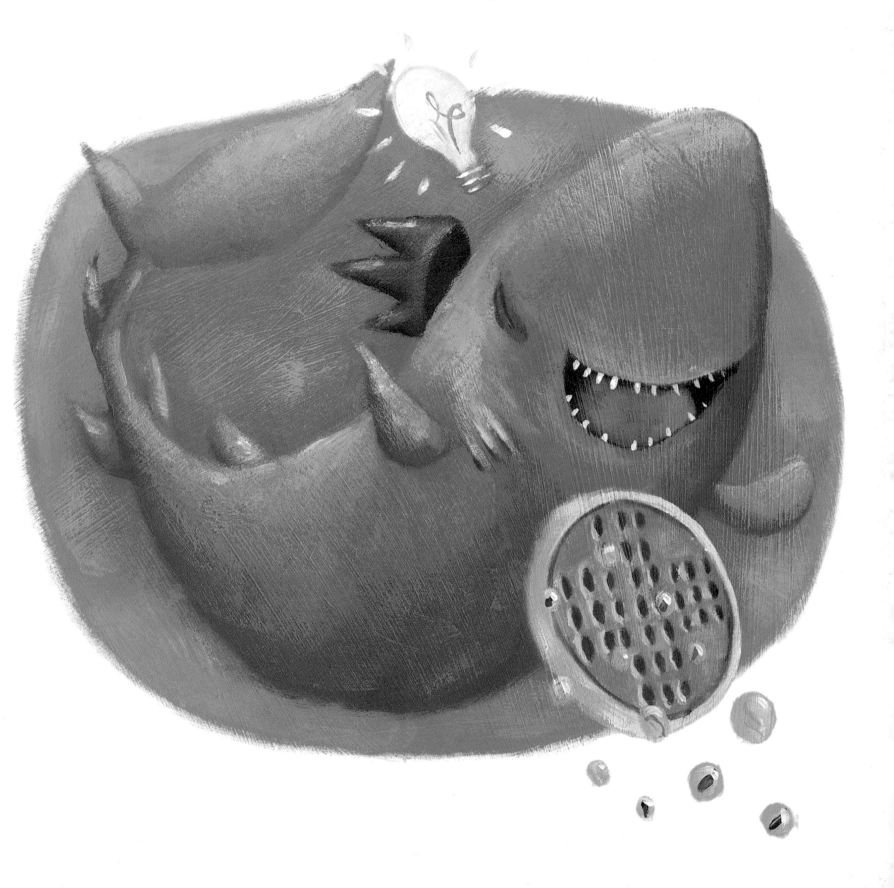

Claude went into his kitchen and started busily

mixing and **stirring** and

rolling and

whisking and

waited . . .

. . . then **iced.**

When it was finished, Claude swam
to the party with what he had made.

'You made this?' sang the fish.
'But it's the most magnificent cake. It must have taken ages!'
'It was no bother,' said Claude. 'I enjoyed doing it.'

Claude joined in the celebrations . . .

. . . singing

The next day when the sea creatures set about their gardening chores, Claude was around to help.

Not hoeing

or pruning

or planting

or watering . . .

. . . but making tea.

Enjoy more great picture books from Bloomsbury ...

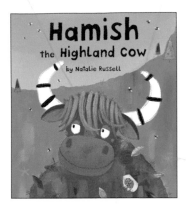

Hamish the Highland Cow
Natalie Russell

Hector the Hermit Crab
Katie Boyce

Also illustrated by Jill Newton for Bloomsbury ...

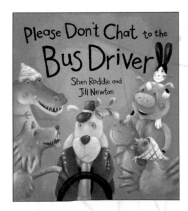

Please Don't Chat to the Bus Driver
Shen Roddie and Jill Newton

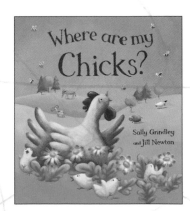

Where Are My Chicks?
Sally Grindley and Jill Newton